The BIG Book of Native American Activities

By Carole Marsh

Editor: Jenny Corsey
Graphic Design & Layout: Cecil Anderson and Lynette Rowe
Cover Design: Victoria DeJoy

Published by

GALLOPADE™
INTERNATIONAL

800-536-2GET
www.gallopade.com

Gallopade is proud to be a member of these educational organizations and associations:

The National School Supply and Equipment Association (NSSEA)
National Association for Gifted Children (NAGC)
American Booksellers Association (ABA)
Association of Partners for Public Lands (APPL)
Museum Store Association (MSA)
Publishers Marketing Association (PMA)
International Reading Association (IRA)

Native American Heritage™ Series

The Native American Heritage Coloring Book

The Best Book of Native American Biographies

Celebrating Native American Heritage: 20 Days of Activities, Reading, Recipes, Parties, Plays, and More!

Mini-Timeline of Awesome Native American Achievements and Events

State Indians: A Kid's Look at Our State's Chiefs, Tribes, Reservations, Powwows, Lore and More From the Past and the Present!

Available for all 50 states!

Native American Heritage Readers™

Black Hawk	Tecumseh	Sitting Bull
Chief Powhatan	Sacagawea	Geronimo
Pocahontas	Sequoyah	Crazy Horse
Ben Nighthorse Campbell		

African American Heritage Series: Black Jazz, Pizzazz, & Razzmatazz™

12 Exciting Products!

Hispanic Heritage Series: Fiesta! Siesta! & All the Resta!™

6 Exciting Products!

③

A Word From the Author

Dear Kids,

    Native American heritage is a very special history. Almost everything about Native Americans is interesting and fun! This group of people shares a remarkable past that helped create the great nation of America. Native Americans are unique and have accomplished many important things for our country.

    This Activity Book is chock-full of activities to motivate you to learn more about Native Americans. While completing puzzles, coloring activities, searching through word finds, and other fun activities, you will learn more about Native American heritage, geography, history, people, places, and more.

    Whether you're sitting in a classroom, riding in the backseat of a car, or doing pages for fun in your room, I hope that you have as much fun using this Activity Book as I did writing it!

    Enjoy learning about Native American heritage – it's the educational journey of a lifetime!

Carole Marsh

National Historic Landmarks

Use the picture clues to match each Native American historic landmark with its name.

1. Fort Bowie and
   Apache Pass
   Cochise County, Arizona

   _____

2. Mesa Verde
   National Park
   (Cliff Palace)
   Mesa Verde, Colorado

   _____

3. Crazy Horse Memorial
   Black Hills,
   South Dakota

   _____

4. Pompey's Pillar
   Yellowstone County,
   Montana

   _____

5. Serpent Mound
   Locust Grove, Ohio

   _____

A

B

C

D

E

Symbol Scramble

Write the correct number next to each Native American symbol.

_____ basket   _____ moccasins   _____ kachina doll

_____ eagle feathers   _____ bow and arrows   _____ maize

Buzzing Around

Write the answers to the questions below. To get to the beehive, follow a path through the maze.

1. The American _____ were the first people to live in America.

2. The largest Native American _____ is the Cherokee Indians.

3. Sometimes, but not always, Indians live on _____.

4. Native Americans would often sign a _____ with the U.S. government.

5. Cochise and Geronimo were two Apache _____.

6. Native Americans who lived on the Great Plains relied on _____ as a source of food.

7. Shoes made of deerskin or other soft leather are called _____.

8. Sitting Bull was a Sioux (Hunkpapa Lakota) _____ and holy man.

9. Some tribes sent young people out on their own for a _____.

10. Scientists today use _____ to learn about ancient Native Americans.

[Maze with hexagons labeled: Start here, Indians, reservations, tribe, vision quest, treaty, archaeology, warriors, chief, buffalo, moccasins]

ANSWERS: 1.Indians 2.tribe 3.reservations 4.treaty 5.warriors 6.buffalo 7.moccasins 8.chief 9.vision quest 10.archaeology

From One Continent to Another

Scientists think that Native Americans may have traveled from Asia into North America when the Bering Strait was frozen thousands of years ago. Some stayed in Alaska. These were the Aleut and Inuit Indians. Some migrated east into the present-day country of Canada. Others migrated south into lands that became the United States of America.

Use a red crayon to trace a path through the maze.
Color Asia green. Color the United States blue. Color Canada red.

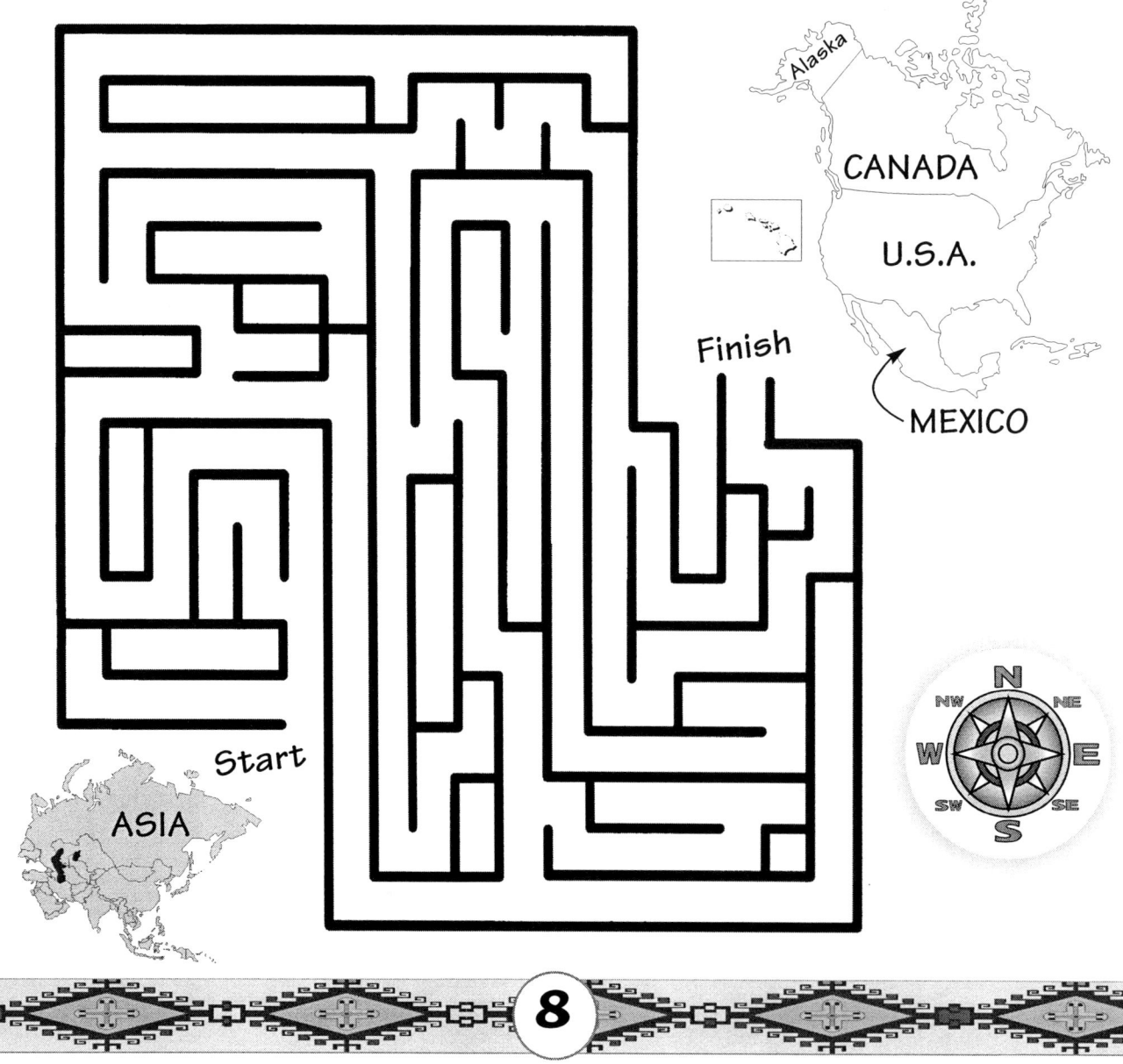

Famous Native American Women

Use the picture clues to match each woman with her description. Each Native American woman listed below was inducted into the National Women's Hall of Fame!

A. Susette La Flesche (1854 - 1903)

B. Wilma Mankiller (1945 -)

C. Sacagawea (1790 - ?)

D. Katherine Siva Saubel (1920 -)

E. Maria Tallchief (1925 -)

F. Annie Dodge Wauneka (1910 - 1997)

G. Sarah Winnemucca (1842 - 1891)

_____ 1. Native American leader who fought to return land taken by the government back to the tribes

_____ 2. Prima ballerina with the New York City Ballet and artistic director for the Lyric Opera Ballet in Chicago

_____ 3. First woman elected to the Tribal Council, worked to improve health practices among her Navajo people

_____ 4. Shoshone woman who served as Lewis and Clark's guide during their exploration of the American West

_____ 5. Member of the Omaha Tribe; worked for Native American rights; first Native American published lecturer, artist and author

_____ 6. Ethnoanthoropologist who founded the first museum run by Native Americans, Malki Museum at the Morongo Reservation in California

_____ 7. First woman elected Principal Chief of the Cherokee Nation.

ANSWERS: 1.G, 2.E, 3.F, 4.C, 5.A, 6.D, 7.B

Campfire Cooking!

Many Native Americans traveled frequently. Cooking had to be quick, tasty, and creative. Native Americans hunted meat, grew vegetables, and gathered berries and herbs.

Indian Pudding

3 cups milk
1/4 cup butter
3/4 tsp. cinnamon

2/3 cup sugar
1 cup milk
2/3 cup dark molasses

3/4 tsp. nutmeg
1 tsp. salt
2/3 cup yellow cornmeal

Heat oven to 300°F. Grease a large casserole dish. Cook 3 cups of milk and the molasses over low heat. In a separate bowl, mix the cornmeal, sugar, salt, cinnamon, and nutmeg. Gradually add this mixture to the hot milk and molasses. Add butter. Cook mixture over low heat, stirring constantly until thickened (about 10 minutes). Pour into the dish. Pour 1 cup milk over pudding and do not stir. Bake dish for three hours. Serve with ice cream or whipped cream!

Wagmiza Wasna
(traditional Sioux snack)

Toast 2 cups of yellow cornmeal in a skillet, stirring constantly so it won't burn. Heat 1 cup of oil in another pan. Grind up 1 cup raisins and mix with oil. After 30 minutes of toasting the cornmeal, mix all the ingredients together with 1/3 cup of sugar. Eat like candy!

Indian Rock Soup

Place three smooth, medium-sized, clean rocks in a large stockpot. Cover with water and bring to a boil. Add 1 large diced onion, 3 large diced tomatoes, 3 peeled and sliced carrots, 1 stalk sliced celery, 1 cup hominy corn, 1 tablespoon butter, 1 teaspoon black pepper, and 1 teaspoon salt. Boil soup until all the vegetables are cooked. Take rocks out of the pot. Serve the soup hot with cornbread!

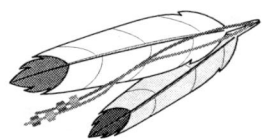
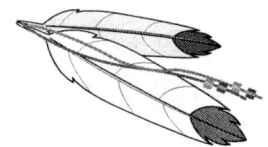

Totem Pole

A totem is an animal that is respected by members of certain American Indian tribes. Some Native Americans believe that they are descended from a totem ancestor, or that they and the totem are "brothers" or "sisters." Many times it may be forbidden to kill or eat the sacred animal. The symbol of the totem may be engraved on weapons, pictured in masks, or (among Native Americans of the Pacific Northwest) carved on totem poles.

Which animal would you choose to represent your family? Design your own totem pole.

Famous Names

How many people do you know that are called by only one name? Many famous Native Americans, who often had many names, were referred to by a single name.

Match the people below with their descriptions.

A. Geronimo

B. Sequoyah

C. Sacagawea

D. Squanto

E. Pocahontas

F. Tecumseh

G. Pontiac

H. Osceola

1. _____ Shoshone guide for Lewis and Clark in the West

2. _____ Fierce Apache war chief

3. _____ Invented the first written Indian language for the Cherokee

4. _____ Legendary Indian princess

5. _____ Great Shawnee warrior who led a famous rebellion

6. _____ Among the first Indians to meet the European explorers

7. _____ Led warriors in the Second Seminole War

8. _____ Ottawa leader who led the Pontiac Rebellion

"I was born on the prairies where the wind blew free and there was nothing to break the light of the sun." –Geronimo

ANSWERS: 1.C, 2.A, 3.B, 4.E, 5.F, 6.D, 7.H, 8.G

12

American Indian Heritage Month

Red Fox James, a Blackfoot Indian, rode horseback from state to state seeking approval for a day to honor Indians. On December 14, 1915, he presented the endorsements of 24 state governments at the White House. In 1990 President George Bush approved a joint resolution designating November 1990 "National American Indian Heritage Month." Similar proclamations have been issued each year since 1994.

Fill in each day of American Indian Heritage Month with an important Native American achievement or event. Some have been done already to help get you started. Celebrate each day of American Indian Heritage Month by remembering these and other important contributions of American Indians!

NOVEMBER

1	2	3	4	5	6	7
Code Talkers serve during World War II.	Indian Arts and Crafts Act of 1990 protects rights of Native artisans.	John Bennett Herrington, of Chickasaw heritage, becomes the first Native American in space.	Pilgrims and Indians share the first Thanksgiving.			
8	9	10	11	12	13	14
15	16	17	18	19	20	21
22 / 29	23 / 30	24	25	26	27	28

Inspiring Puppets

Cut out the faces of these inspirational Indian leaders. Glue them onto craft sticks. Write short speeches for each puppet.

Sitting Bull

Chief Joseph

Geronimo

Sequoyah

Pocahontas

Osceola

Tecumseh

Have a puppet parade!

Indian Cooking Crossword

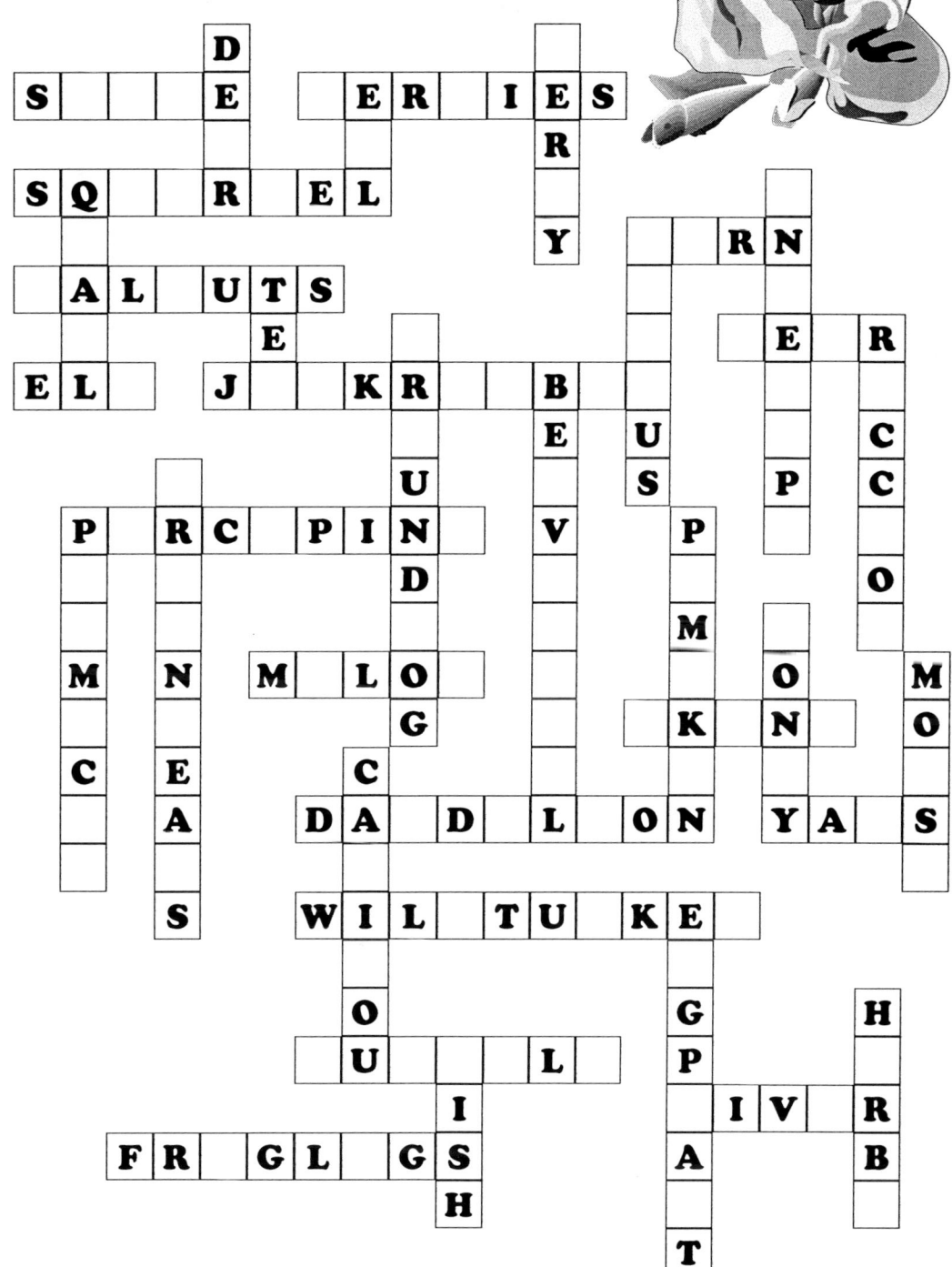

WORD BANK

corn
skunk
pumpkin
melon
green beans
pemmican
walnuts
cactus
wild turkey
buffalo
jackrabbit
beaver tail
elk
antelope
squirrel
fish
groundhog
berries
bear
eel
dandelion
honey
moose
deer
quail
caribou
porcupine
yams
raccoon
tea
snake
frog legs
egg plant
herbs
liver
jerky

Use the Word Bank and letter clues to complete the crossword puzzle.

Native American Proverbs

Unscramble the words below!
Where each proverb originated
from is written in parentheses.

Word Bank

alone		relatives
finger	nature	giver
respect	handsome	eye
fight	prevent	

1. One **NGEFIR** _____ cannot lift a pebble. (Hopi)

2. Most of us do not look as **OMNDEHAS** _____ to others as we do to ourselves. (Assiniboine)

3. He who is present at a wrongdoing and does not lift a hand to **NTEVPRE** _____ it, is as guilty as the wrongdoers. (Omaha)

4. He who would do great things should not attempt them all **ELOAN** _____. (Seneca)

5. With all things and in all things, we are **ELESRATIV** _____. (Sioux)

6. Respect the gift and the **VERGI** _____. (Omaha)

7. Judge not by the **YEE** _____ but by the heart. (Cheyenne)

8. When we show our **RPECTES** _____ for other living things, they respond with respect for us. (Arapaho)

9. It is senseless to **FHTIG** _____ if you cannot hope to win. (Apache)

10. When a man moves away from **TURNAE** _____, his heart becomes hard. (Lakota)

ANSWERS: 1.finger 2.handsome 3.prevent 4.alone 5.relatives 6.giver 7.eye 8.respect 9.fight 10.nature

16

Hard at Work

Match these hardworking Native Americans with their jobs.

Put an A by the seamstress.

Put a B by the nurse.

Put a C by the fabric weaver.

Put an D by the chef.

Put an E by the teacher.

Put a F by the athlete.

Put an G by the soldier.

Put an H by the dancer.

Put a I by the medicine man.

Put a J by the musician.

Native American Matching Game

SUPPLIES

- 15 small index cards (white)
- colored markers or crayons
- scissors
- black permanent pen
- colored construction paper or magazine pictures
- glue or tape

DIRECTIONS

1. Cut each index card in half (the width) to make 30 cards. Arrange the cards into a square on the floor. There should be five cards across and six cards down. Choose a Native American scene. Color the cards so that they will all look like one picture.

2. Use the colored construction paper or magazine pictures to create 15 pairs of Native American symbols. Some ideas for symbols are: eagle, basket, deer, weaving, feather, pottery, campfire, buffalo, arrow, dreamcatcher, shield, quills, teepee, horse, drum, or even a desert sunset.

3. Mix up the 15 icons on the floor. Randomly choose an icon to glue onto the back of each index card. The colored picture part should be on top, and the symbol clue will be on the other side. Let the glue dry.

4. Turn the cards over and play the matching game with a friend. Each player takes a turn to choose two cards and try making a match. If a player chooses two cards that don't match, they are replaced. The player with the most matches wins!

> Ask an adult to laminate the cards so they will last longer! Store the cards in a plastic bag for future games.

18

Build A Dream Catcher

Dream catchers originated in traditional American Indian beliefs. They protected a baby by catching everything evil, like a spider's web catches and holds everything that comes in contact with it. Evil forces included colds, illness, and bad spirits. According to legend, "If you believe in the great spirit, the web will catch your good ideas — and the bad ones will go through the hole."

Materials

- 5 inch ring
- 4 yards suede lacing
- 3 yards waxed nylon string
- Beads
- Feathers
- Scissors
- Glue
- Clothes pin

Note: This is just one way to make dream catchers. No two ever look exactly the same. See how many different ones your can make!

DIRECTIONS

1. Wrap the suede lacing around the ring until you reach the starting point again. Glue the ends of the lacing to the ring. Hold it in place with a clothes pin until the glue dries.

2. Make the web using the imitation waxed nylon string and tying it to the ring.

3. Hang your dream catcher using a 12-inch piece of suede lacing. Tie the ends together to form a loop. Slip the loop end through the ring and then around the ring and over the knot.

4. Tie pieces of suede lacing on each side of the ring. Slip 3 beads onto each piece of lacing and secure each with a knot. Push feathers up inside the beads on each piece of lacing. Glue the feathers if they are loose.

Bolting Buffalo

The buffalo provided many Native Americans with almost everything they needed to live. Indians usually tried to use as much of the animal as possible so nothing would be wasted.

hides: clothing, storage bags, blankets

fat: soap, candles, cooking grease

bones: tools, arrowheads

bladders: storage containers

hair: ropes, pillow stuffing

hoofs: glue, wind chimes

meat: cooking, dried jerky

horns: spoons, bowls

tendons: bow strings

dung: fuel, fertilizer

blood: paint

intestines: cord

teeth: ornaments, jewelry

tongue: considered to be a delicious delicacy

Study the six buffalo below. Circle the two buffalo that look exactly the same.

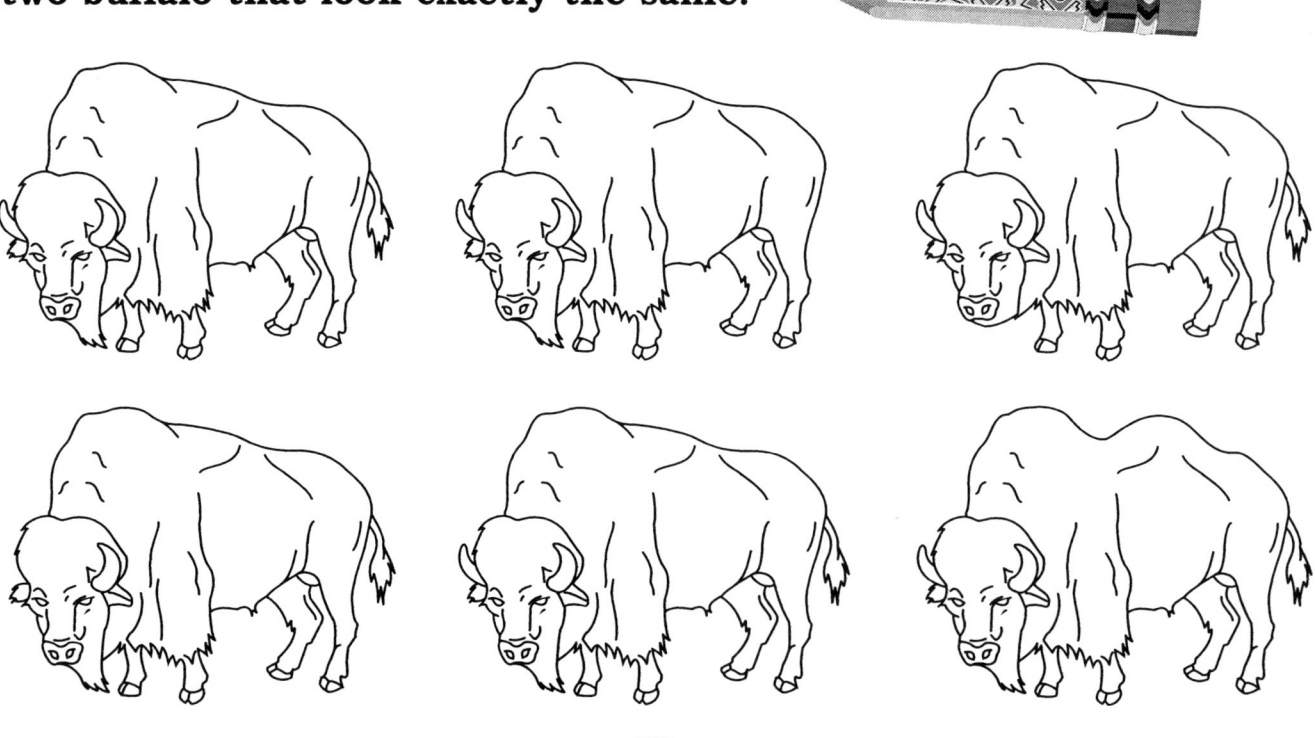

20

Sacagawea

Sacagawea was a young Shoshone Indian woman who guided Meriwether Lewis and William Clark during their exploration of the West. She helped them find wild roots, berries, and medicines in nature when the expedition party was near starvation. She interpreted Indian language and culture so Lewis and Clark could meet with native peoples along the way. She even convinced her Shoshone relatives to help the explorers cross the Rocky Mountains. The Lewis and Clark party might have faced starvation and death or been lost in the wilderness if Sacagawea had not helped them.

In 2000, the United States issued a special one-dollar coin bearing Sacagawea's image to honor her accomplishments. Color the coin.

Sacagawea gave birth to Jean Baptiste Charbonneau on the journey. William Clark nicknamed him "Pompy" because he was always dancing around!

21

Say That Again?

During the Maritime Fur Trade, Russia, England, France, and many Indian nations wanted to trade together. However, none of their traders knew everyone else's language! They created a form of communication called Chinook Jargon using words from all the languages. This way they could do business together without having to learn four or five new languages!

Find the meaning of each Chinook Jargon word by holding this page up to a mirror. Sound out each word. Write the meanings on the lines below.

1 kah cole chako
The North

_____

2 tumtum
heart

_____

3 cole
cold

_____

4 potlach
give

_____

5 wawa
a speech

_____

6 tyee
chief

_____

7 saghalie
heaven

_____

8 tupso
grass

_____

9 yaka
who

I am a "tyee!"

ANSWERS: 1. The North; 2. heart; 3. cold; 4. give; 5. a speech, 6. chief; 7. heaven; 8. grass; 9. who

Pull Apart Nature Prayers

Native Americans worshiped and respected nature. They wanted to be unified with the nature. They offered long and short prayers about nature to the Great Spirit, a god.

"Pull apart" these Native American prayers. Write the sentences on the lines below.

1. Ihearthesoundofthewindandlfeelfree.

_____

2. Seethebirdsupinthesky.HowIwishthatIcouldfly.

_____

3. Asmyeyessearchtheprairie,Ifeelthesummerinthespring.

_____

4. GreatSpirit,Iopenmyarmstoearthlybeauty. Thesongofthetreessingssoftlyinmyheart.

_____

5. TheSpiritoftheMoonlightsmytravel.OfwhomshallIbeafraid.

_____

23

Native American...

A cultural region is a geographical region where different Indian tribes had similar ways of life. The culture areas are a system of classification used to organize tribes.

Arctic — The Inuit people are native to the Arctic region. The Aleut people inhabit the Aleutian Islands near Alaska's southwest coast.

California — Most California Indians lived in tules (like a teepee made of stiff plants) and were famous for their basketry. Some of these tribes included Hupa, Chumash, Pomo, Miwok, Wintun, Yahi, and Maidu.

Great Basin — The Great Basin Indian tribes lived in bowl-shaped lowlands between the Rocky Mountains and the Sierra Nevada. Tribes included the Shoshone, Paiute, Ute, and Bannock.

Great Plains — Some Great Plains tribes were Sioux, Cheyenne, Crow, Hidatsa, Osage, Pawnee, Omaha, Tonkawa, Comanche, and Arapaho.

Northeast — The Northeast Indian tribes farmed the land and used wood from the forest to build their homes. These peoples included the Iroquois, Algonquian, Susquehannock, Powhatan, Roanoke, Sac, Fox, Pequot, Seneca, Shawnee, Lenape, and many others.

Northwest — The Northwest Indians hunted elk, gathered berries, and fished for food. These tribes included the Chinook, Makah, and Nootka.

Plateau — This region is full of rivers and streams for fishing and is covered in tall evergreen forests. These tribes included the Walla Walla, Modoc, Klamath, Nez Perce, Yakama, Spokan, and others.

Southeast — The Southeast Indians were skilled farmers. The Cherokee, Catawba, Creek, Alabama, Seminole, Chickasaw, Choctaw, and other tribes lived here.

Southwest — Pueblo, Apache, Navajo, Hopi, and other tribes lived in the Southwest. Today the Navajo, one of the largest tribes in the United States, live on the largest reservation.

Subarctic — The Subarctic region has evergreen forests and huge lakes. These tribes include the Carrier, Chipewyan, Kutchin, Cree, Montagnais, and Naskapi.

Cultural Regions

Color the map
using the
Color Code.

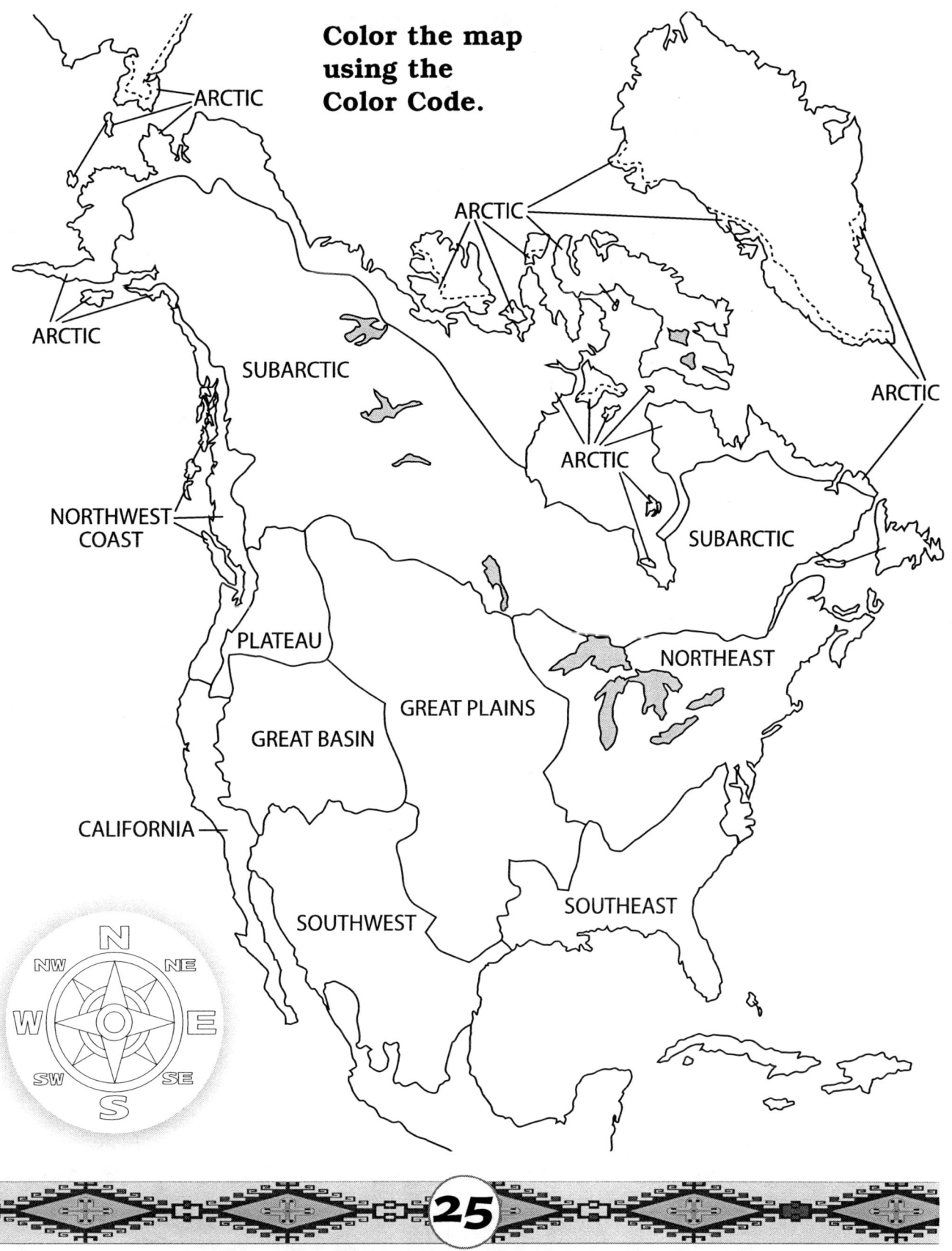

ARCTIC

ARCTIC

ARCTIC

ARCTIC

SUBARCTIC

ARCTIC

SUBARCTIC

NORTHWEST
COAST

PLATEAU

NORTHEAST

GREAT PLAINS

GREAT BASIN

CALIFORNIA

SOUTHEAST

SOUTHWEST

N
NW   NE
W   E
SW   SE
S

25

Native American Collage

SUPPLIES
● piece of white or colored poster board
● magazines, catalogs, newspapers, postcards, etc.
● glue
● scissors

DIRECTIONS

1. Browse through magazines, catalogs, newspapers, postcards, and whatever else you can find. Look for pictures of Native American people, tribes, locations, symbols, history, events, anything that looks interesting. Cut out several pictures until you have a large pile.

2. First spread out all the pictures on the poster board. See what looks best together. It's okay if some parts overlap. How can you arrange it differently so more pictures show?

3. When you have decided where the pictures should go, glue each one to the poster board. Design a Native American border with pieces of colored construction paper. Hang the collage in your room!

Don't use too much glue. A light coat is more than enough. Too much glue will make the picture look wet, then wrinkled when it dries.

26

Indian Legends

Native American history is full of legends, stories, and myths. These come from their oral tradition. This is when people pass down their history through the generations by speaking instead of writing.

Read the Indian legend. Circle the nouns. Underline the verbs. Write your own legend in the space below. Continue writing on another sheet of paper if you need more room.

How The Wildcat Got Its Spots (Shawnee Story)

Once a wildcat chased a rabbit. When he almost caught him, the rabbit darted into a hollow tree. The wildcat sat outside the tree and waited until the rabbit got hungry and had to come outside. Finally, the rabbit said he would come out and be eaten if the wildcat would roast him on a fire. He did not want to be eaten raw! The wildcat eagerly built the fire. When the sticks had burned down to coals, the rabbit suddenly jumped out and struck his powerful feet into the coals! They flew at the wildcat and burned out little spots of hair. The rabbit escaped! Later, when the hair grew again, it was white. This is why the wildcat has white spots on its breast.

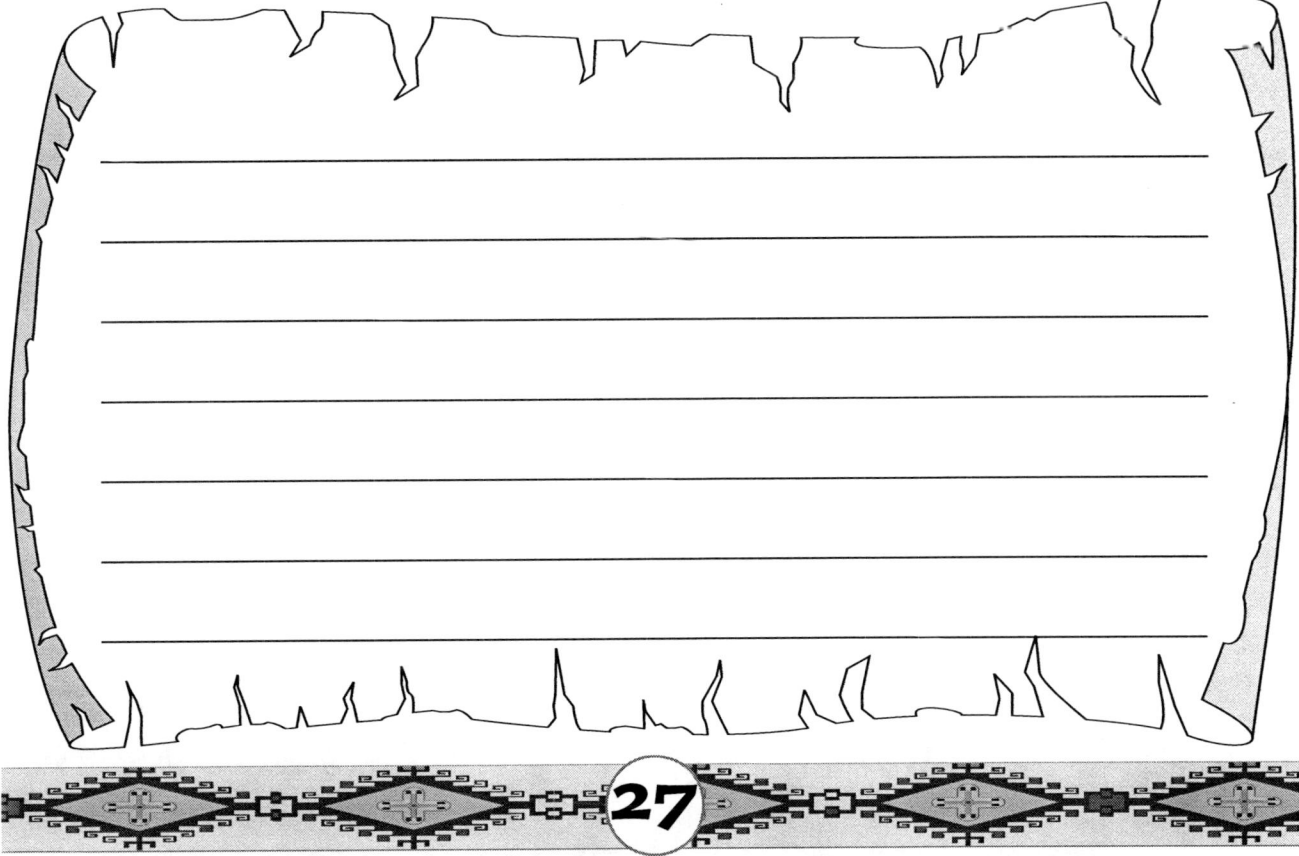

Navajo Code Talkers

The U.S. Marines wanted to send secret messages about war strategies, but they didn't want their enemies to read them. They needed a code. A Navajo engineer named Philip Johnston had an idea. He suggested that Navajo soldiers should send the messages in their native language! The Marines recruited 29 young Navajo men to create the code. Their work was so successful that eventually more than 400 Navajo Code Talkers were recruited!

Each letter is represented by a Navajo word in the official Code Talker Alphabet below. Decipher the secret message!

A	wol-la-chee	ant	J	tkele-cho-gi	jack	S	dibeh	sheep
B	shush	bear	K	klizzie-yazzie	kid	T	than-zie	turkey
C	moasi	cat	L	dibeh-yazzie	lamb	U	no-da-ih	Ute
D	be	deer	M	na-as-tso-si	mouse	V	a-keh-di-glini	victor
E	dzeh	elk	N	nesh-chee	nut	W	gloe-ih	weasel
F	ma-e	fox	O	ne-ahs-jah	owl	X	al-an-as-dzoh	cross
G	klizzie	goat	P	bi-sodih	pig	Y	tsah-as-zih	yucca
H	lin	horse	Q	ca-yeilth	quiver	Z	besh-do-gliz	zinc
I	tkin	ice	R	gah	rabbit			

In which war did the Navajo Code Talkers serve?

_____	_____	_____	_____	_____
gloe-ih	ne-ahs-jah	gah	dibeh-yazzie	be

_____	_____	_____
gloe-ih	wol-la-chee	gah

_____	_____	_____
than-zie	gloe-ih	ne-ahs-jah

Memorize the code and send secret messages to your friends!

The First Thanksgiving

In the fall of 1621, the Pilgrims shared the first Thanksgiving feast with Chief Massasoit and 90 of his Wampanoag warriors at Plymouth. This event was an Indian tradition designed to thank God for a good harvest. The Wampanoag were patient and kind to the Pilgrims when they first arrived in the New World. They taught the colonists how to farm and helped them survive the first winter.

Color the Thanksgiving scene shared by the Indians and Pilgrims.

29

Famous Chiefs

There are countless famous chiefs in Native American history. These wise men led their tribes bravely through the American conquest of their land.

Match each chief with his tribe from the word bank.

WORD BANK	Sac and Fox	Crow	Hunkpapa Lakota Sioux
	Blackfoot Confederacy	Nez Perce	Oglala Lakota Sioux

1. Chief Sitting Bull _____

(Hint: Which tribe sounds like a handsome daddy?)

2. Chief Joseph _____

(Hint: Could this chief have had a pierced nose?)

3. Chief Red Cloud _____

(Hint: Tribal initials in alphabetical order are LOS.)

4. Chief Plenty Coups _____

(Hint: Which tribal name is also the name of a bird?)

5. Chief Crowfoot _____

(Hint: If your feet were dirty, you might call them this.)

6. Chief Blackhawk _____

(Hint: This tribal name contains the name of a "sly" animal.)

ANSWERS: 1-Hunkpapa Lakota Sioux; 2-Nez Perce; 3-Oglala Lakota Sioux; 4-Crow; 5-Blackfoot Confederacy; 6-Sac and Fox

Eagle Paper Bag Puppet

SUPPLIES
- lunch-size brown paper bag
- colored markers or crayons or paints
- black, yellow, and white construction paper
- gluestick
- scissors

DIRECTIONS

1. Close the paper bag and lay it flat (opening side down, fold on top). Cut an eagle-shaped head from white construction paper. Color the edges with black marker to give it feathers. Glue the head on top of the flap. It should stick up over the top, but not below the flap.

2. Cut a curved beak shape from yellow construction paper. Cut two eye circles from white construction paper and give it black eyeballs. Glue the beak and eyes on the eagle head.

3. Cut a rectangle from black construction paper to fit the front of the paper bag. Glue the rectangle "body" under the flap on top of the bag.

4. Cut out a right and left wing from black construction paper. Make them as big as you like. Glue the tips of the wings on the upper sides of the flattened paper bag, inside the folds.

5. Cut out either a tail flap (as shown) or several tail feathers from white construction paper. Glue these just under the top section of the paper bag at the bottom. Cut out six small ovals from yellow construction paper. Glue three "claws" on each side, overlapping the black rectangle body and white tail feathers. Lay a heavy book on the eagle to help it dry flatter. Play with your eagle puppet!

> If you don't have any paper bags, you could attach your eagle puppet to a paint stirrer stick, a wooden chopstick, or an unsharpened pencil.

Craft Crossword

Indians are well known for their beautiful arts and crafts, including rawhide shields, ceremonial masks, leather dolls, beaded moccasins, quillwork, carved totem poles and house posts, even wooden sleds. Many Indians shaped clay into intricately painted and engraved pottery. Textile crafts include finger weaving, twining and plaiting, crocheting and knitting, loom weaving, and clothing. Baskets were plaited, twined, or coiled.

Use the word bank of "craft materials" to solve the crossword.

WORD BANK

clay	dyes	quill	beads
wood	leather	antlers	silver
bark	stone	bone	copper
shells	feathers	horn	fur
gourd	hair	rawhide	grass

Some Indians even used sea lion whiskers and porcupine tails for their crafts!

Indian Names

Indians were often named for animals or places found in nature. Some tribes traditionally named a child for the first thing the mother saw outside her home after giving birth.

Look at each picture. Write a creative Indian name under each line that fits with the picture.

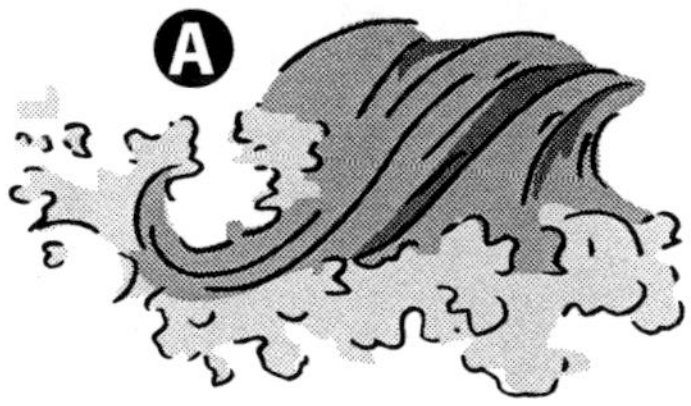

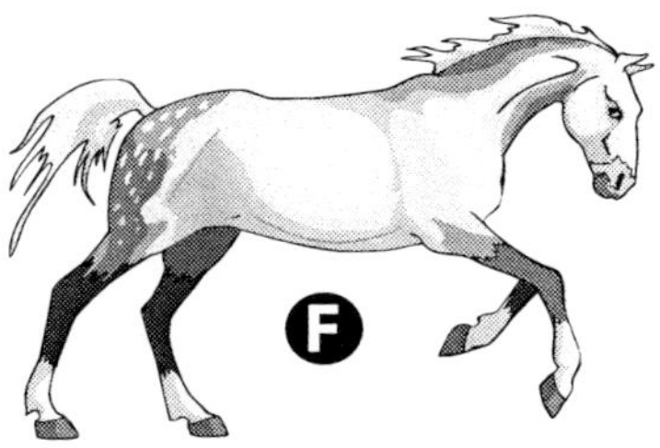

A. _____

B. _____

C. _____

D. _____

E. _____

F. _____

G. _____

H. _____

Answer Suggestions: A. Water Runs Rough; B. Running Buffalo; C. Standing Elk; D. Looking Bear; E. Hunting Wolf; F. Spotted Horse; G. Perched Hawk; H. Sun In Sky

Great Plains Teepee

Trace the half-circle pattern onto brown paper and cut out. Then decorate it with Indian symbols, pictures, buttons, leaves, anything! Roll the paper into a cone and tape the inside edges shut. Cut a small slit from the bottom and fold back to make a doorway. Glue some toothpicks in the small hole at the top.

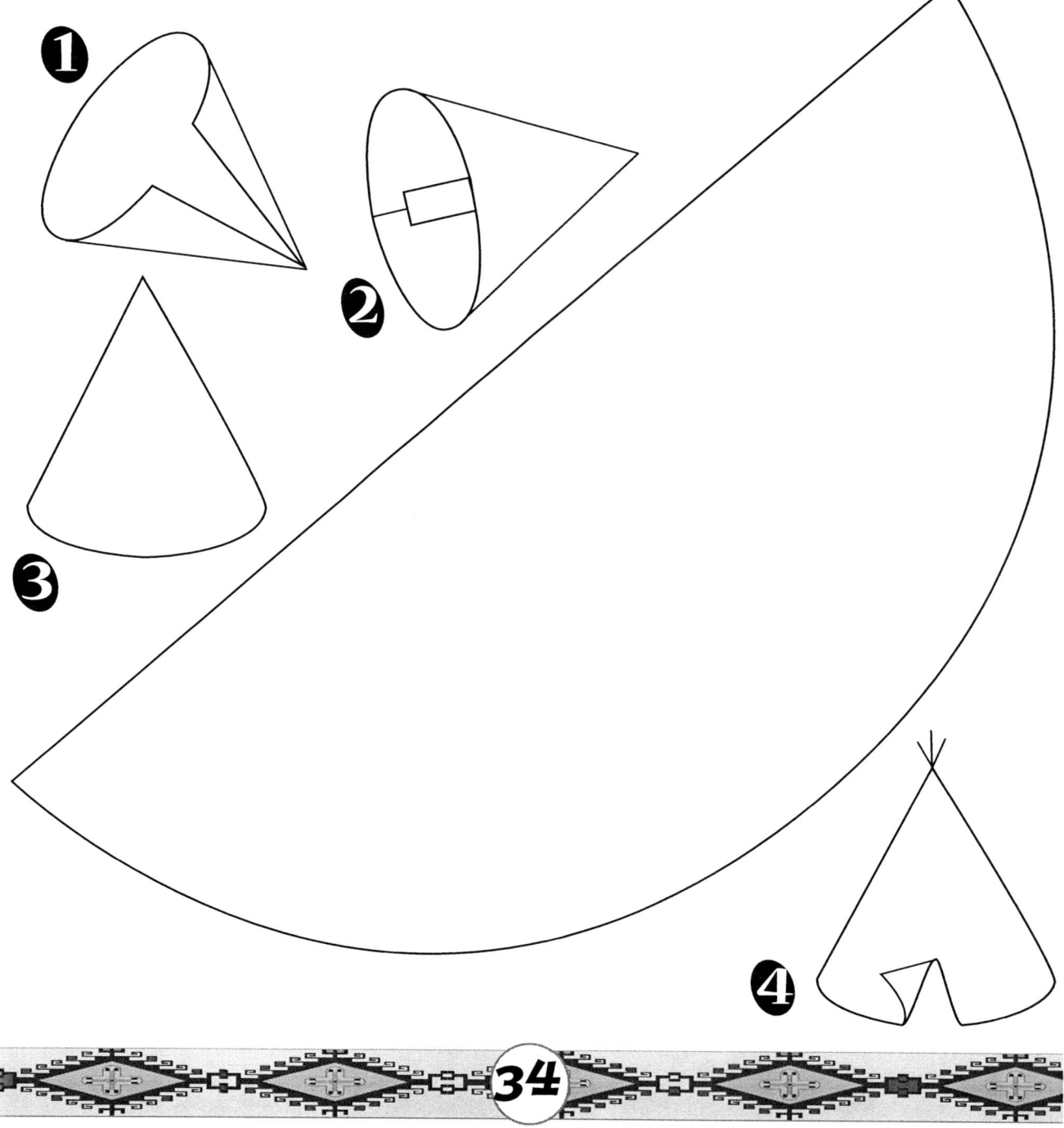

Home Sweet Home

North American Indian families lived in many different kinds of homes. Each dwelling was built with materials found in the family's region. The homes also were built to protect the family from the weather common to their region, such as sizzling sunshine or blistering blizzards. **Label each Indian home correctly.**

	WORD BANK
wickiup (Apache)	teepee (Plains Indians)
longhouse (Iroquois)	igloo (Inuit)
pueblo (Pueblo Indians)	chickee (Seminole)

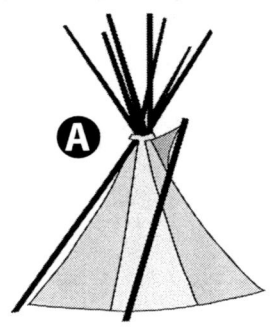

A. _____

B. _____

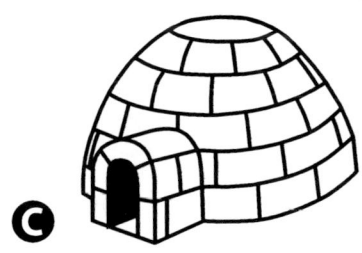

C. _____

D. _____

E. _____

F. _____

Answer: A. teepee; B. pueblo; C. igloo; D. longhouse; E. chickee; F. wickiup

Five Civilized Tribes

The Five Civilized Tribes were friendly Indians that developed trade relations with the Europeans. These Indians, who mostly lived in the Southeast, even adopted some of the European customs.

During the Civil War, both the Union and Confederacy asked the Indians to fight with them. The Indians could not decide which side deserved their loyalty. Some went to the Confederacy. Some went to the Union. More than 10,000 Indians died. Many survivors lost homes and fields when armies set them afire. After the war ended, 14 Indian tribes signed a peace contract to never again fight with each other.

The U.S. government wanted to punish the Indian "rebels" who had fought for the Confederacy. They forced the Five Civilized Tribes, who had all sided with the Confederacy, to sign peace treaties which included selling their Western lands. Eventually each of these five tribes was forced to relocate to Indian Territory, a government reservation. The people suffered greatly as they walked the long distance to their new home. Many died during this "Trail of Tears."

Solve the code to find out the names of the Five Civilized Tribes.

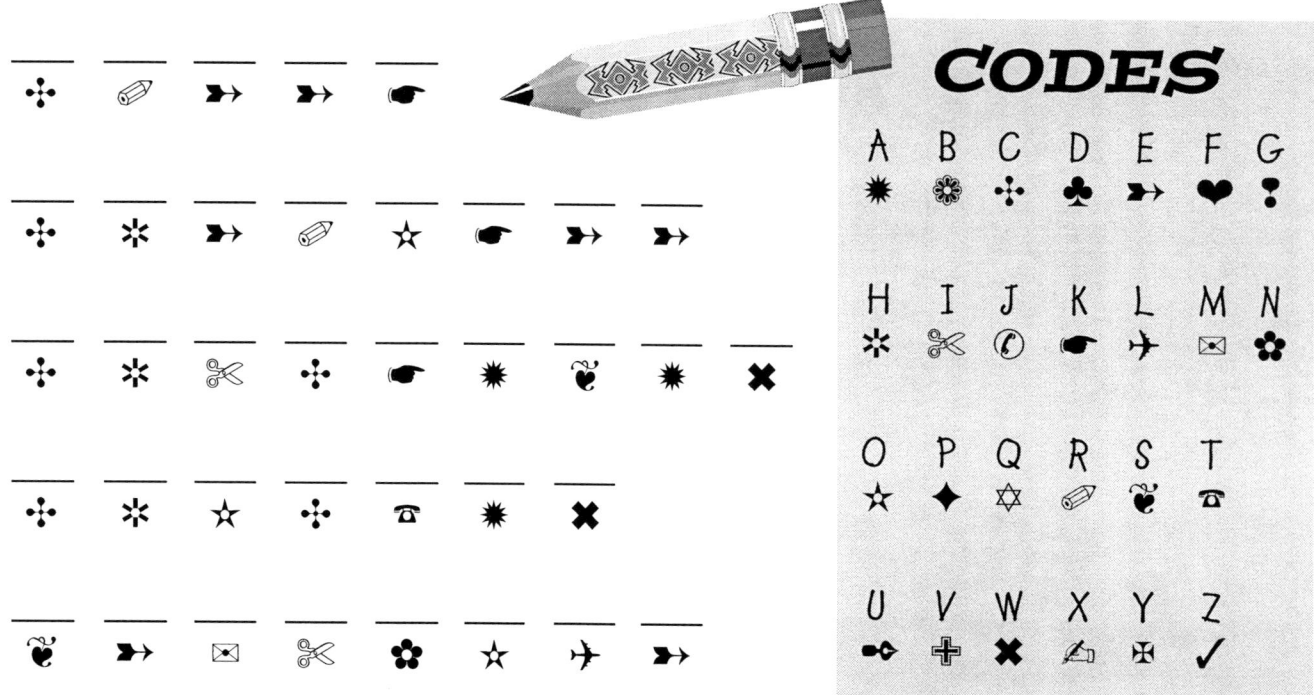

CODES

Answer: Creek, Cherokee, Chickasaw, Choctaw, Seminole

Native American Word Wheel

1. Navajo Indians drew paintings from _____ to help cure the sick.

2. The Plains Indians wore _____ into battle.

3. Eastern Woodland Indians made beaded _____ to store healing herbs.

4. Northwest Coastal Indians built _____ to display before their homes.

5. Algonquian Indians made _____ to give their children good dreams.

6. Pueblo children played with _____, which represented their gods, so they would not be afraid.

WORD WHEEL

- kachina dolls
- dreamcatchers
- totem poles
- war bonnets
- medicine bags
- sand

Answer: 1. sand, 2. war bonnets, 3. medicine bags, 4. totem poles, 5. dreamcatchers, 6. kachina dolls

A Look at Lacrosse

Most all of Southeastern Indian tribes played a ball game from which the modern game of lacrosse was adapted. Wooden sticks with a pocket of laced deerskin were used to hurl deerskin balls to teammates in an effort to travel down the field and score into the goal.

Answer the following questions about the game of lacrosse.

_____ 1. If both teams have ten players, how many players are on the field in total?

_____ 2. If a goalkeeper's crosse is 72 inches, and a players crosse is 52 inches, what is the difference in length?

_____ 3. How many quarters are in a game of lacrosse? (Hint: How many quarters make up a whole?)

_____ 4. If a lacrosse team has two timeouts per half, how many timeouts can a team call in one game (no overtime)?

_____ 5. If a player gets a 1 minute penalty for an illegal body-check, and has served 37 seconds, how many more seconds must the player wait?

Make a Wampum Necklace!

The Eastern Algonquians and Iroquois used wampum for special ceremonies. They made wampum from seashells — mostly the quahog clam. The shells were shaped into white or purple beads by grinding them into cylindrical shapes. Wampum belts were used as tribal records and to remember special events. Wampum beads became a highly prized trade item. Later, Dutch and English settlers traded glass beads with the Indians in exchange for other goods.

You can make your own wampum necklace using colored pasta and string. Thread the pasta onto a long piece of string and tie.

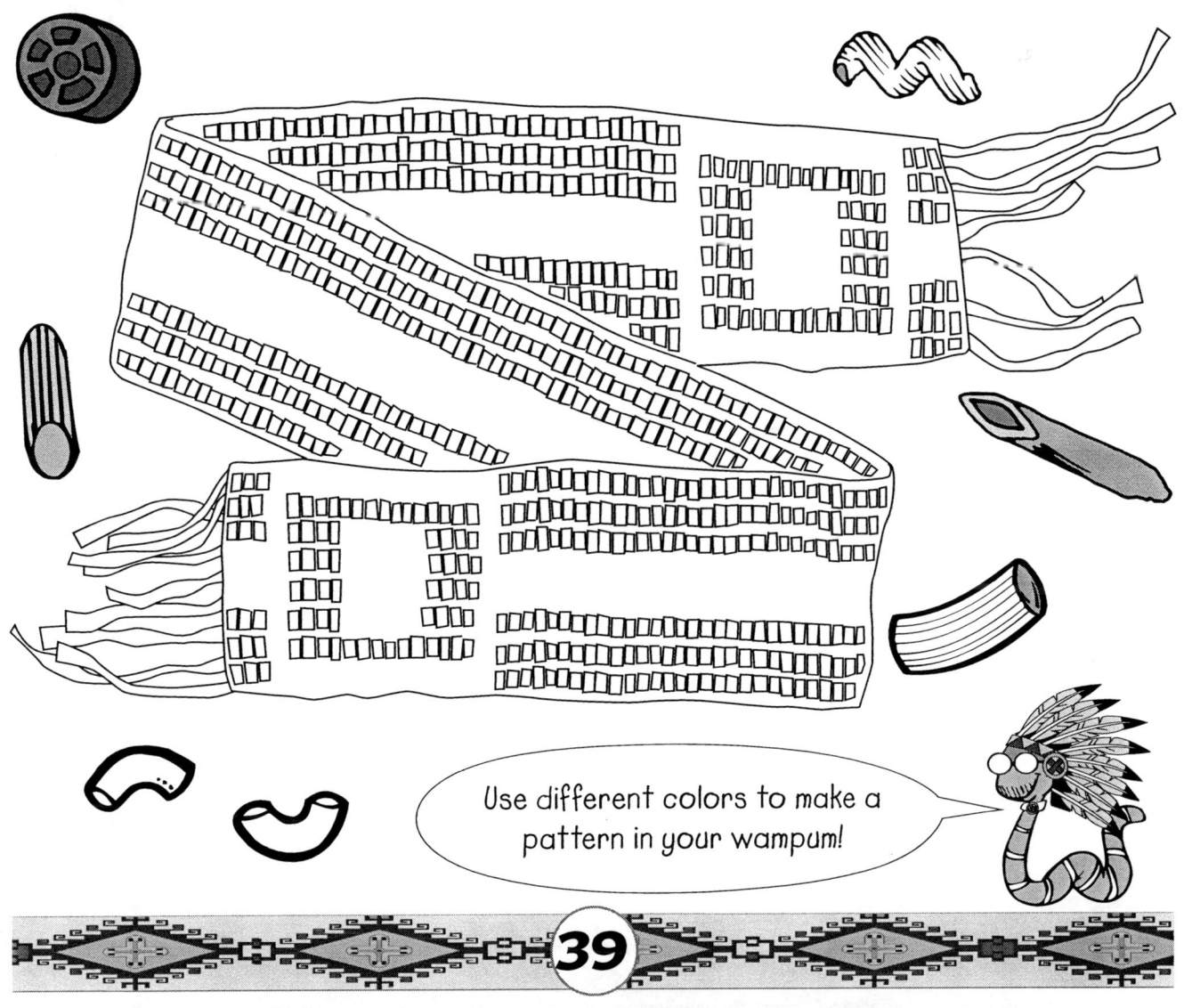

Use different colors to make a pattern in your wampum!

Color Me!

Native American

BLUE — Blue like the great sky that covers the world.

YELLOW — Yellow like rippling rows of fresh maize.

RED — Red like bright war paint before battle.

ORANGE — Orange like warm sunsets over the plains.

PURPLE — Purple like hazy mountains in the west.

GREEN — Green like the silent trees in the forest.

Quick Quote Quiz

Read the quotes. What do you think about each one? Do you agree or disagree? What is the speaker trying to communicate? Write your responses below.

"One does not sell the earth upon which the people walk." — Crazy Horse (Lakota)

_____

_____

_____

"My heart is very strong." — Satanta (Kiowa)

_____

_____

_____

"It is our great desire and wish to make a good, permanent peace." — Little Raven (Arapahoe)

_____

_____

_____

"Our land is worth more than your money." — Blackfeet chief to U.S. negotiators in the 1850s

_____

_____

_____

Native Americans in Government

Write the correct abbreviation next to the senator or representative from that state.

U.S. SENATE

____ 1. Hiram R. Revels, Lumbee from Mississippi, 1870–1871

____ 2. Mathew Stanley Quay, Abenaki or Delaware from Pennsylvania, 1887–1899 and 1901–1904

____ 3. Charles Curtis, Kaw from Kansas, 1907–1912 and 1915–1929

____ 4. Robert L. Owens, Cherokee from Oklahoma, 1907–1925

____ 5. Ben Nighthorse Campbell, Northern Cheyenne from Colorado, 1993–2004

U.S. HOUSE OF REPRESENTATIVES

____ 6. Charles Curtis, Kaw from Kansas, 1893–1907

____ 7. Charles D. Carter, Choctaw from Oklahoma, 1907–1927

____ 8. W.W. Hastings, Cherokee from Oklahoma, 1915–1921 and 1923–1935

____ 9. Will Rogers, Jr., Cherokee from California, 1943–1944

____ 10. William G. Stigler, Choctaw from Oklahoma, 1944–1952

____ 11. Benjamin Reifel, Rosebud Sioux from South Dakota, 1961–1971

____ 12. Clem Rogers McSpadden, Cherokee from Oklahoma, 1972–1975

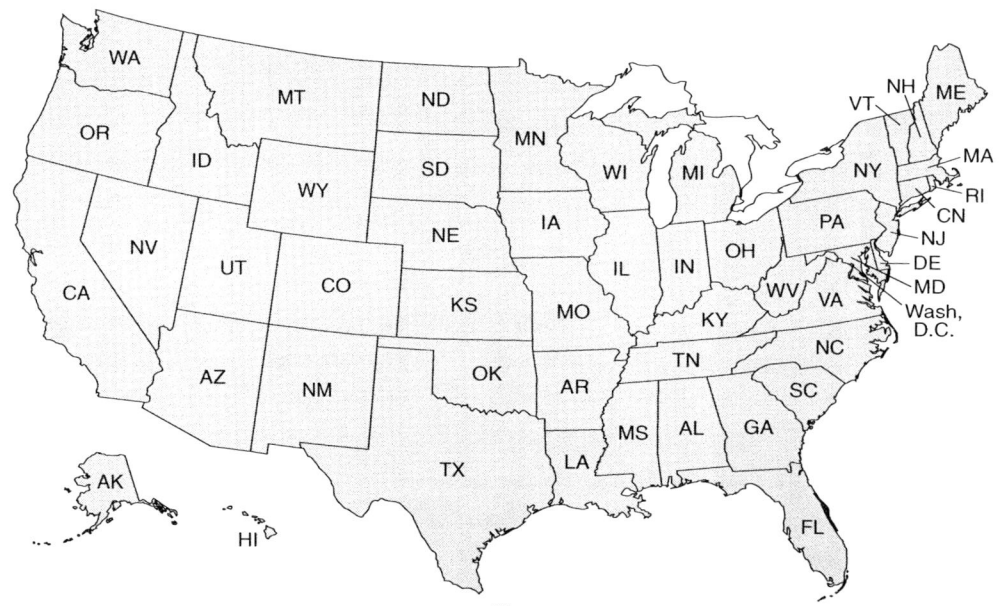

Here and Now

Study the two maps. Think about the information they provide. Answer the questions below.

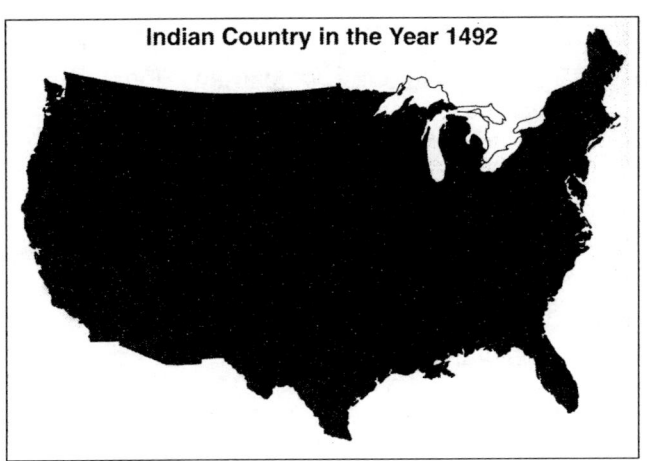

Indian Country in the Year 1492

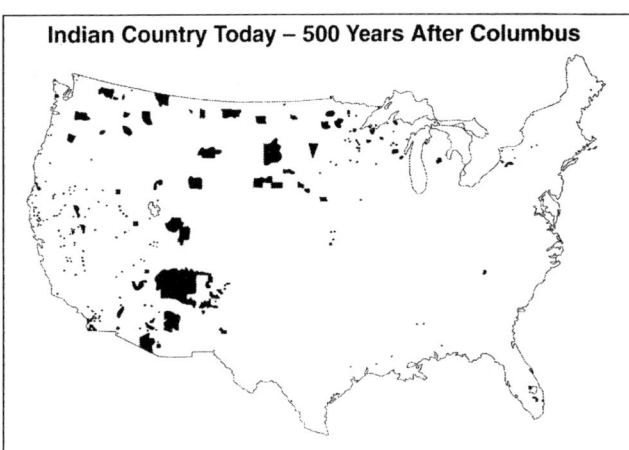

Indian Country Today – 500 Years After Columbus

1. Do tribes have more or less land today than they did in the 1400s? Why?

   _____

   _____

2. Did the U.S. government acquire Indian Territory honestly? If not, how was it taken?

   _____

   _____

3. Would it be possible to give the land back to the Indians today? How is history irreversible?

   _____

   _____

43

Eastern Native American Tribal Word Search

Find each tribe in the word search below.

NORTHEAST: Abenaki, Cayuga, Chippewa, Fox, Huron, Illinois, Iroquois, Kickapoo, Lenni Lenape, Mahican, Maliseet, Massachuset, Menominee, Miami, Micmac, Mohawk, Mohegan, Montauk, Narragansett, Nipmuc, Oneida, Onondaga, Ottawa, Passamaquoddy, Pennacook, Penobscot, Pequot, Potawatomi, Powhatan, Roanoke, Sac, Seneca, Shawnee, Susquehannock, Tuscarora, Wampanoag, Wappinger, Winnebago

SOUTHEAST: Alabama, Apalachee, Caddo, Calusa, Catawba, Cherokee, Chickasaw, Chitimacha, Choctaw, Coushatta, Creek, Lumbee, Natchez, Seminole, Timucua, Tunica, Yamasee, Yazoo, Yuchi

```
T U C I C A C H I P P E W A N A T C H E Z
U C H S A A M A B A L A E E N W A H S E C
S A O E C O U S H A T T A N L C R E E K H
C M C C A L U S A A P A L A C H E E N S I
A C T S U S Q U E H A N N O C K L S E W T
R I A P F O X M A S S A C H U S E T C I I
O M W O O W L T O C S B O N E P N P A N M
R L W T N A R R A G A N S E T T N E S N A
A U A A O M G N A N M M E N O M I N E E C
L M S W N P K I C K A P O O C A L N M B H
H B A A D A W P P E Q U O T A L E A I A A
A E K T A N A M C H U R O N T I N C N G R
N E C O G O H U L A O F A S A S A O O O O
T N I M A A O C N O D T O A W E P O L A A
I A H I L G M D Z T D D T C B E E K E B N
M G C S E E S A M A Y N O A A T S D K E O
U E D N P F Y U C H I S P O W H A T A N K
C H E R O K E E R E G N I P P A W O M A E
U O I L L I N O I S N E C M O N T A U K P
A M A H I C A N M I A M I I R O Q U O I S
R C A Y U G A T U N I C A R O N E I D A R
```

Western Native American Tribal Word Search

Find each tribe in the word search below.

NORTHWEST COAST: Chinook, Haida, Makah, Tlingit, Tsimshian

PLATEAU: Cayuse, Coeur d' Alene, Flathead, Kalispel, Klamath, Kootenai, Modoc, Nez Perce, Palouse, Spokan, Umatilla, Wallawalla, Yakama

CALIFORNIA: Chumash, Hupa, Maidu, Miwok, Pomo, Wintun, Yahi, Yokuts, Yurok

GREAT BASIN: Bannock, Paiute, Shoshone, Ute

SOUTHWEST: Apache, Havasupai, Hopi, Hualapai, Mohave, Navajo, Papago, Pima, Pueblo, Yaqui, Yavapai, Yuma, Zuni

GREAT PLAINS: Arapaho, Arikara, Assiniboine, Blackfeet, Cheyenne, Comanche, Crow, Gros Ventre, Hidatsa, Ioway, Kaw, Kiowa, Mandan, Missouria, Omaha

Osage, Otoe, Pawnee, Ponca, Quapaw, Sioux, Tonkawa, Wichita

```
P  A  I  U  T  E  S  H  O  S  H  O  N  E  C  A  Y  U  S  E  N
A  T  O  N  K  A  W  A  P  A  M  O  O  G  A  P  A  P  F  C  A
L  C  H  U  M  A  S  H  E  E  N  N  E  Y  E  H  C  O  L  H  V
O  Y  U  R  O  K  T  C  C  I  H  A  Y  U  M  A  O  N  A  I  A
U  E  P  U  E  B  L  O  R  C  R  O  W  A  I  K  M  C  T  N  J
S  M  A  K  A  H  M  E  E  N  W  A  P  N  G  I  A  A  H  O  O
E  K  H  A  V  A  S  U  P  A  I  L  U  I  S  W  N  W  E  O  T
A  L  I  O  W  A  Y  R  Z  B  S  Z  O  M  O  I  C  A  A  K  I
R  A  D  I  A  H  R  D  E  S  I  M  V  I  U  C  H  L  D  A  G
A  M  A  W  E  U  B  A  N  N  O  C  K  W  R  H  E  L  B  L  N
P  A  T  A  G  O  T  L  M  P  U  Y  M  O  I  I  O  A  L  I  I
A  T  S  P  A  E  Q  E  A  D  X  W  A  K  A  T  A  W  A  S  L
H  H  A  A  S  S  I  N  I  B  O  I  N  E  O  A  R  A  C  P  T
O  F  N  U  O  U  T  E  D  W  A  N  D  E  C  M  I  L  K  E  S
O  I  U  Q  A  Y  O  K  U  T  S  T  A  U  N  I  K  L  F  L  P
M  M  O  H  A  V  E  W  I  N  T  U  N  G  W  P  A  A  E  M  O
A  P  A  M  A  K  A  Y  E  R  T  N  E  V  S  O  R  G  E  O  K
H  T  S  I  M  S  H  I  A  N  K  O  O  T  E  N  A  I  T  D  A
A  P  A  C  H  E  W  K  A  W  I  A  P  A  L  A  U  H  H  O  N
A  L  L  I  T  A  M  U  Y  A  V  A  P  A  I  T  S  R  P  C  W
```

Canoe Racing!

Help Running Deer paddle his canoe safely down the river to get home!

Amazing Native Americans!

Acrostic poems are composed by writing a word or phrase that starts with each letter of a word. See if you can write your own acrostic poem about Native Americans below.

Next to every letter, write a word or phrase that describes Native American people. The first letter is done for you. Now let's see what you can do!

N atural and pure!

A _____

T _____

I _____

V _____

E _____

A _____

M _____

E _____

R _____

I _____

C _____

A _____

N _____

S _____

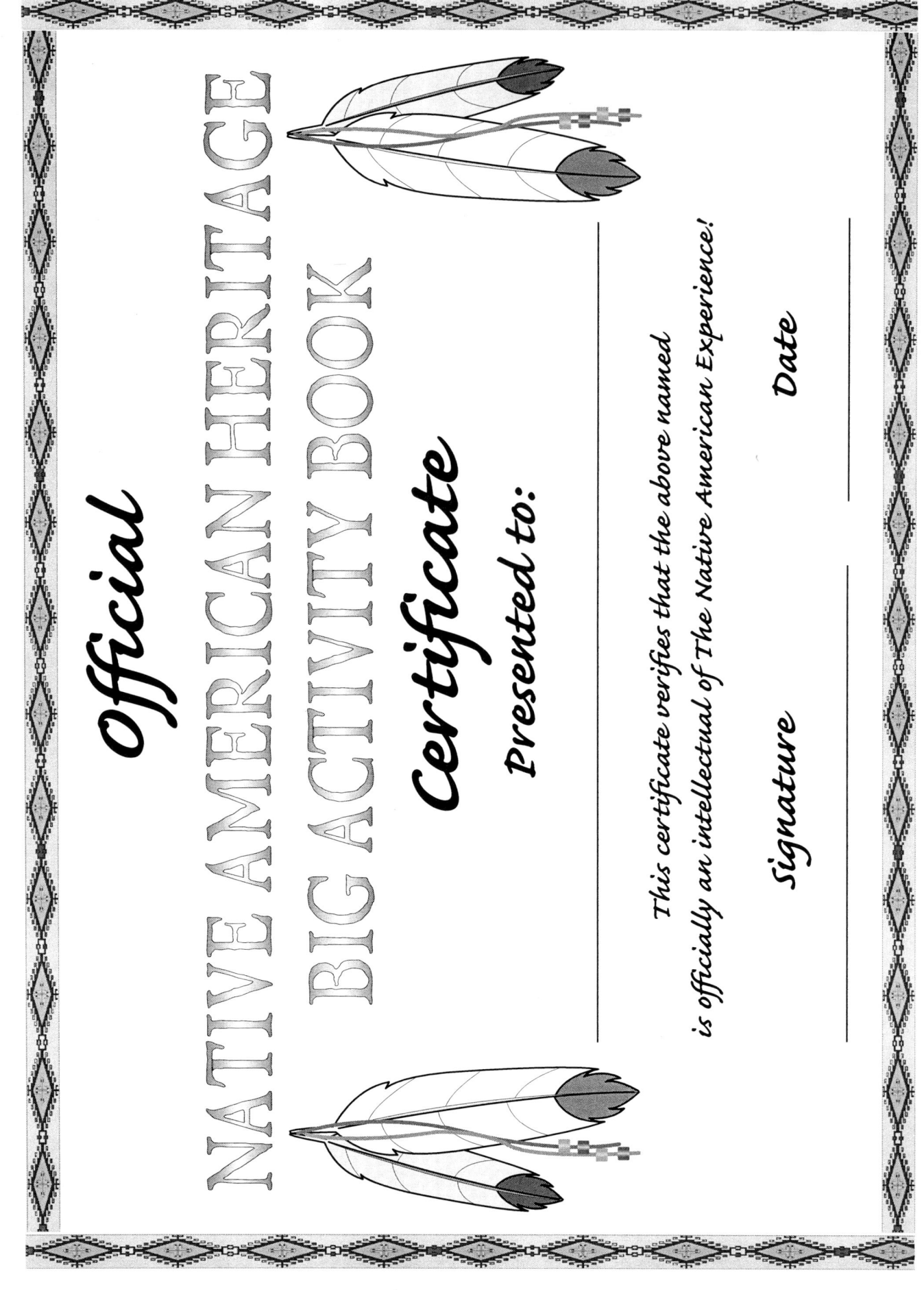

Official

NATIVE AMERICAN HERITAGE
BIG ACTIVITY BOOK

Certificate

Presented to:

_____

This certificate verifies that the above named
is officially an intellectual of The Native American Experience!

_____
Signature

_____
Date